Darla's Hair

Justin Duff

Illustrated by Lizzy Love

ISBN: 978-1-68222-094-8

Darla's Hair Project

Dalra's Hair helps support children and their families during a difficult transition into a new struggling chapter of their lives. Not every child is a victim but all peadatric cancer warriors can be a hero. Times like these children need strength, love and support. Darla's Hair Project help families cope easier knowing others are lifting them up at a time of feeling so low. Darla's Hair Project helps bring awareness to the subject of Childhood Cancer and the importance of awareness. With awareness we can help motivate a method and one day help create a cure. We also help families struggling finacially with home away from home costs. Nothing is more appreciated then not having to worry about minor priorities but focusing on helping our children over come this battle and remaining brave. For further details check out our website **www.booksbyjustinduff.com.**

Darla once had beautiful hair,

Until she was diagnosed with cancer.
Darla had to shave her head.

This made Darla very sad.
Until her mom came home
With a humongous box.

Now Darla has red hair

And green hair.

She has orange hair,

Yellow hair,

Pink hair,

Purple hair

And blue hair.

Sometimes Darla has long hair,

Or short hair,

Or straight hair

Or curly hair.

Sometimes Darla has her hair up,

And sometimes she has her hair down.

Darla is the happiest Darla around.